For CHJ and JHS

Other titles by Clare Jarrett:
Catherine and the Lion
Dancing Maddy

First published in hardback in Great Britain by HarperCollins Publishers Ltd in 2001

1 3 5 7 9 10 8 6 4 2
ISBN: 0-00-198414-4

Text and illustrations copyright © Clare Jarrett 2001
The author/illustrator asserts the moral right to be identified as the author/illustrator of the work.

The HarperCollins website address is: www.**fire**and**water**.com

Printed in Singapore

JAMIE

Clare Jarrett

Collins

An imprint of HarperCollinsPublishers

One stormy evening a strange bird walke
through the gate and up the path.

"What's that tapping sound?" asked Jamie.

Grandfather opened the door.

"My goodness me!" he said to the bird.
"You must be freezing with no feathers or
coat. Come in."

Jamie fetched some towels. "We must get
him warm and dry," he said.

"He looks hungry," said Jamie.

"Do you think he'll eat spaghetti?" asked Grandfather.

"Worms would be better," said Jamie. He put his coat on and went out to find some.

The bird was very hungry.

"He needs a name," said Grandfather.

Jamie looked around at his toys. "How about Thomas?" he said.

"My father's name was Thomas," said Grandfather. "What do you think, Thomas?"

The bird looked up. "Chirp," he said.

"Where will Thomas sleep?" Jamie asked.

Grandfather rummaged about in a cupboard.

"Here we are!" he said at last. "Not too big and not too small."

"And he can have my old jumper," said Jamie, tucking it into the box.

Thomas settled himself in and was soon fast asleep.

In the morning they took Thomas to the vet.

"He needs to be checked over, and we need some advice," said Grandfather. "I've never looked after a bird before."

"Mmm," said the vet. "He'll be fine. Plenty of good food, fresh air and exercise."

They bought a large bag of food, a special bowl and some seeds.

"Seeds will make his feathers grow glossy and strong," said Grandfather.

"So he *will* grow some?" asked Jamie.

"Oh yes," said Grandfather, "given time."

Thomas soon felt at home. He liked to help around the house. But sometimes he got in the way.

One evening during supper Thomas landed in the butter, by accident.

"Oh dear," said Grandfather, in dismay. "I think he needs his own house," said Jamie. "Chirp," said Thomas.

Later that night, Thomas sat on Grandfather's head. Grandfather woke up with a start.

"Thomas," he said, "this is *too* much."

He got up, went downstairs, and started to draw a plan for Thomas' house.

The next day
Grandfather and
Jamie collected bits
of wood, nails,
tiles and paint.
Thomas helped as
much as he could.

He found a chimney pot.
"I don't think you'll
need that," said Jamie.

"But these will be very useful," said
Grandfather, pulling out a set of wheels.

At last the house was finished. Jamie stood by, while Grandfather got his camera ready for the grand opening. Off came the sheet.

Flash! went the camera.

Thomas walked up and down the ramp, crowing and chortling.

"He likes it!" shouted Jamie.

"Quite right," said Grandfather, "I wouldn't mind living there myself."

The next time Jamie came to stay with Grandfather, Thomas had changed.

"Oh, Thomas, what beautiful feathers," said Jamie.

Thomas puffed himself up so that his feathers glistened and shone in the sunlight.

"Chirp, chirp, chirrup," said Thomas.

"Oh, yes," said Jamie, "and I've missed you too."

"It's time for a
photograph," said
Grandfather.

Suddenly there was
a terrible commotion.
"Chirp, *pock-pock-pock*,
chirp, chirrup, *pock*."

"Go and see
what's bothering
Thomas, Jamie,"
said Grandfather.

Jamie peered into the little house. "Thomas!" he cried. "I didn't think you could do that."

"Well I never," said Grandfather. "He's laid you a beautiful, brown egg."

"Grandfather," said Jamie seriously, "Thomas is a girl."

"We'll just have to call him Thomasina then," said Grandfather.

"*Pock-pock-pock*, chirrup, *pock*," said Thomas.